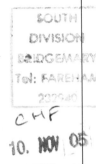

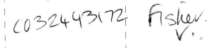

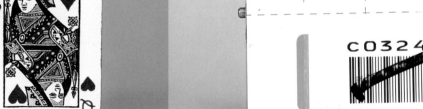

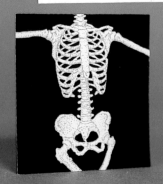

ELLSWOr

extraor

electric

BY VALORIE FISHER

TH'S
DINary
ears

and other
amazing
alphabet
anecdotes

SIMON &
SCHUSTER

SIMON & SCHUSTER, LONDON

First published in Great Britain in 2003
by Simon & Schuster UK Ltd
Africa House, 64-78 Kingsway,
London WC2B 6AH

Copyright © 2003 by Valorie Ann Fisher

Originally published in 2003 by
Atheneum Books, an imprint of
Simon & Schuster Children's
Publishing Division, New York.

A CIP catalogue record for this book
is available from the British Library
upon request.

Book design by Lee Wade.
The text for this book is set in Filosofia.

Manufactured in China

ISBN 0689837364

10 9 8 7 6 5 4 3 2 1

acknowledgments

For their superbly silly suggestions in this enormously
enjoyable endeavour, I give thanks to my son, Aidan; my
mum and dad, Susan and Jim Fisher; Karen Hatt; Matt
Mitler; and Barbara Ensor. I thank my daughter, Olive,
for blithely believing she is obeying the "yust yook-
ing" rule, and my husband, David, for his exceptional
expertise in electrifying ears. And I give great gobs of
gushing gratitude to Anne Schwartz and Lee Wade for
their wondrous wealth of wit and wisdom.

Alistair had an alarming appetite for acrobats.

Betty believed in a big but balanced breakfast.

Carleton's curious carousel captivated
the colourful carnival crowds.

Dot dreamed of driving a delightfully dainty dump truck.

Ellsworth's extraordinary electric ears
were endlessly entertaining.

Fancy feathered fashions were favoured
by Floyd's farm friends.

Gwendolyn's good-looking gorillas were great gardeners.

Holly was hugely happy in her humble handbag home.

It's incredible! Igor's invisible ice cream was irresistible.

Josie joined Judy on a jittery, jerky, jolly jaunt on her jackrabbit.

Kyle's kids kept kites in the kitchen.

Lucy's lopsided laundry line was loaded
with long and loopy letters.

Mario's mechanical moustache machine made many mistakes.

Nigel's nifty newspaper neckties were
nothing but a naughty nuisance.

Otis often observed ostriches on opening night at the opera.

Pepita's pink paper parasols were particularly popular with pirates. Perfectly puzzling!

Quentin quickly quieted the quibbling, quarrelling, and quacking of the quintuplets.

Ruby was really rather remarkable at refrigerator rocket repairs.

Supermarket-salad snacking was Stanley's summer sport.

Trust Trevor to tell you, typing on a trapeze was terribly tricky.

Uncle Upton's unusual utensils were unbreakable,
unforgettable, and utterly useless.

Visiting the valley of a violent volcano
was very invigorating for Violet.

Wilbur worked wonders with wallpaper.

Xanthia's X ray explained her exuberance.

Yates yelled, "Yippee for Yellow!"

Zelda's zigzagged zebra was the zippiest at the zoo.

can YOU FIND THESE aLPHaBET OBJECTS in eacH PICTURE?

A

acrobat
aeroplane
alligator
apple
apple tree
ants
armadillo

B

baby
ball
ballerina
balloon
banana
baseball player
bat
bathing suit
beach
bear
beet
beverage
birthday cake
blue
blueberry
bottle
bread and butter
breeches
bucket
burger

C

cabbage
cap
camel
card
carnival
carousel
carrot
caterpillar
cheetah
chicken
chimpanzee
clock
cloud
clown
construction worker
corn
cow
cowboy
crab
crane

D

daisy
dice
dinosaurs
dirt
dog
dove
driver
duck
dump truck

E

ear
elephant
emu
envelope
eye

F

farm
feathers
fence
flashlight
foals
fowl
fox
frogs

G

gaggle of geese
galoshes
garden
gate
giraffe
goose
grapes
green

H

hair
handbag
handle
hat
head
heart
hoe
hog
hood
hoof
horse
hose
house

I

iguana
Igor's Invisible Ice Cream

J

jaguar
jewellery
jungle
Jupiter

K

kangaroos
ketchup
kettle

key
kitchen
kites
kitty
koalas

L

ladder
ladybird
laundry basket
laundry line
lawn
lawn mower
leg
lemon
lemon tree
letters
limb
lion
lizard
llama
locomotive
lollipop
LUCKY

M

machine
meerkats
monkey
moon
moose
moustaches
mouth

N

99
neck
necktie
nest
newspaper
nose
number

O

opera
opera glasses
ostriches
OTHELLO
owl

P

paintbrush
panda
pants
paper
parasols
parrot
pavement
pear
peas
pencil
penguin
people
PEPITA'S

pink
pirates
plates
purple

Q

Quail Quarterly, The
Queen Bee, The
QUIET
Questionable Quotes
Quilt or Quit?
*Quintessential
    Quince, The*
quintuplets
Quirky Queens

R

rabbit
raccoon
radio
rake
red
refrigerator rocket
rhinoceros
ribbon
robot
rock
roller skates
rooster
rope
ruler

S

salad
salamander
sand
seashell
shopping cart
shovel
skunk
snake
soap
soccer ball
soup can
spaghetti
spider
starfish
stegosaurus
strawberry
sugar
sunflower
supermarket
swimsuit/shorts

T

tail
teeth
tent
thumb
tiara
tiger
tightrope
tightrope walker
time
top hat
trapeze
trunk
tutu
two
typewriter

U

umbrella
underwear
unicycle
utensils

V

vendor
violin
Visiting Vesuvius
volcano

W

wagon
wallpaper
watering can
watermelon
wheel
wheelbarrow
white
window
window box
windowpane
wood

X

Xanthia
Ximenes
X ray
X-ray

Y

yard
yellow
yellow jacket
yo-yo

Z

zebra
Zelda's Zoo
zeppelin
zigzags
zookeeper